S0-BAF-188

OMG...
I DID IT
AGAIN?!

Talia Aikens-Nuñez

TO MY DAUGHTER,
WHO INSPIRES ME EVERY DAY

Copyright © 2016 Talia Aikens-Nunez
Cover and internal design © 2016 Central Avenue Marketing Ltd.
Illustrations: Alicja Ignaczak

All rights reserved. No part of this book may be used or reproduced in any manner whatsoever without written permission from the author except in the case of brief quotations embodied in critical articles and reviews.

This is a work of fiction. Names, characters, places and incidents either are the product of the author's imagination or are used fictitiously and any resemblance to actual persons, living or dead, business establishments, events or locales is entirely coincidental.

Published by Central Avenue Publishing, an imprint of Central Avenue Marketing Ltd.
www.centralavenuepublishing.com

Published in Canada
Printed in United States of America

1. JUVENILE FICTION/Fantasy & Magic 2. JUVENILE FICTION / Girls & Women

Library and Archives Canada Cataloguing in Publication

Aikens-Nuñez, Talia, author
    OMG...I did it again?! / Talia Aikens-Nuñez.

Illustrations by Alicja Ignaczak.
Issued in print and electronic formats.
ISBN 978-1-77168-034-9 (paperback).--ISBN 978-1-77168-035-6 (epub).--
ISBN 978-1-77168-052-3 (mobipocket)

    I. Ignaczak, Alicja, illustrator II. Title.

PZ7.A27Om 2016   j813'.6   C2015-907438-X
                                         C2015-907439-8

ONE

"**AHHH!**" April Appleton sat up in bed and let out a gasp. *Breathe. Breathe.* Her chest went up and down from her heavy breathing.

Boom, Boom, BOOM, BOOM! The noise was getting louder and louder. The closer it came, the more her bed shook.

Is that an earthquake? Is there construction going on? Is that thunder? What is that?

Her whole body vibrated with each 'boom'. Her clock banged against the wall. The framed pictures bounced and danced on her desk. Her posters flipped and flapped on the wall.

She threw her legs off the bed and jumped up. Scurrying to look out her bedroom window, there she saw it. The lump in her throat grew. *One, two, three, four,* then she stopped counting. She saw them marching down the street. They were larger than they were in her dream. But they were the exact same color. Huge, grey, wrinkled elephants were marching down the street.

She grabbed her cell phone from the desk. She jumped back into her bed and pulled the comforter over her head, as if that would stop what was happening outside.

She swallowed hard. With her fingers shaking she typed:

TO: Eve LaRue, Grace Galapagos

She squeezed her eyes tightly together, and

hoped this was still a dream. She pinched herself. *Ouch. This isn't a dream.*

Then, memories flashed before her eyes. She remembered Googling a spell to turn her pestering older brother, Austin, into a dog. Then him teasing her on the bus. *Poof.* The spell worked! She panicked and texted Grace, her best friend who was in fifth grade with her. Grace knew Eve, a new student in school who moved to their town from New Orleans. Eve told April about her grandma who also had magical powers. Eve gave April her *Book of Magie*, her spell book. April remembered using her powers to turn Austin back into an angry, red-faced boy. It all came back to her. *OMG... I am a witch*! Her breath quickened.

The loud footsteps of the elephants grew louder and louder. And everything shook more and more.

She opened her eyes and exhaled. Still

under her comforter, the sun streamed through the large pink polka dots. She blinked hard just to make sure all this was real.

With the phone close to her face, she typed:

"OMG... I did it again?!"

With a whoosh, the door to her bedroom opened. She hit the send button.

Holding her breath, she peered over the top of the covers. Austin stood in the doorway with his arms crossed and glaring at her. His foot was tapping. He walked into her room and closed the door behind him. April slowly pulled the covers down to show her face.

His eyes locked on the cell phone. He stomped over to April, grabbed it out of her hands and read the most recently sent message.

"I knew it!" he yelled at her. "You did this," he said pointing out the window at the ele-phants. "You did it AGAIN!"

TWO

"AUSTIN, please don't yell. Mom and Dad might hear you," April pleaded. She was breathing heavily.

Her cell phone rang. April grabbed the phone back. *Please be them. Please be them.* She looked at the screen:

'Grace calling...'

"It's Grace, see?" April extended her arm to show the phone to Austin. "She and Eve will help me fix this."

Her hands quivered as she answered the phone, "Hello?"

"So you're the reason the circus is going down the street, huh?" Grace said with her typical sarcasm.

"Oh, sweet pea, you did it again, huh?" Eve asked, with her sing-songy Southern accent. They had their phone on speaker. But April pressed her phone tightly to her ear.

April hung her head low. Her eyes filled with water. As a tear fell, Austin came closer to her. He put a hand on her shoulder. She lifted her head and wiped the tears away.

"I know you can fix this. You fixed me and you can fix this," Austin said looking into her eyes. His voice was much calmer and lower.

"Even your former furball brother knows you can fix this," Grace said with a chuckle. April cracked a smile.

Austin glared at the cellphone. "What did Grace say?"

April cleared her throat. "She said that was really sweet, what you said."

"I didn't say that," Grace spoke louder. "I said, he'd better watch out or you could turn him back into a FURBALL!"

Austin reached out to grab the phone. April stepped backwards to avoid his reach. "Wait a minute, you two. We have to fix this—not fight. Austin, can you go keep Mom and Dad busy? Grace and Eve, where are you guys?"

"We're at Grace's house. Remember, we were all going to meet at the park? My mom dropped me off earlier this morning," Eve said.

"That's right! The whole elephant thing kinda threw me off this morning," April was talking really fast and throwing her left arm in the air. She started to pace.

"I know this whole being a witch thing is

dramatic, but, save the drama for yo mama," Grace said with attitude.

"If you were in my situation you would be freaking out too!" April quipped back.

Eve jumped in, "Whoa, whoa, girls, girls. We have to stick together and then we will figure out how to handle this. April, sweet pea, start from the beginning and explain, how exactly did you do this?"

THREE

THUD! *Thud! Thud!* The steps of the elephants were coming closer and closer. Everything in April's room was bouncing and vibrating. "Well, it all started when I was—" April started.

"April! Austin! Kids, where are you!" April's mom screamed up the stairs.

April stopped speaking. April and Austin

froze. Austin's eyes bulged. April held her breath.

"April?" Eve asked. "Where did you go?"

"I'm here," April whispered. "My mother is calling me and Austin. What should we do?"

"OK. Here's the plan. Tell Austin to stall your parents. April, you grab the spell book. I think we left it under your bed. Bring it over here and then Eve will help us find a spell to fix this. And, you can tell us how you did this. OK?" Grace sounded determined.

"Sounds good. See you soon," April said as she hung up the phone. "Austin, you go stall mom and dad. I am going to bring the *Book of Magie* over to Grace's so Eve can help me read it to find a spell to fix this." She grabbed her book bag and put in the spell book and her cell phone. Slinging the bag over her shoulder, she grunted.

April looked at Austin. His face was pale.

His mouth was slightly open and he looked like he was having trouble breathing. She held Austin's hands. She swallowed hard.

"Austin, we can fix this. I know we can. I just need your help. I need you to go downstairs and distract Mom and Dad. I will text Mom reminding her that I am going to Grace's. I'm going to sneak downstairs and go out the back door."

"OK. I can do that," Austin sighed. He walked out of April's room. "Mom!" he yelled. "I'm right here. What's going on?" Austin ran down the stairs to meet his mother who was in the kitchen.

April scurried out her door and peered over the hallway banister. She looked down the stairs. She heard Austin talking super fast to their mother. April smiled. She ran back into her room and closed the door.

She walked over to her bed and put her

book bag on it. She opened it and found her cell phone. She texted:

"Mom: I'll be at Grace's."

She hit 'Send'.

April quickly tossed the phone back into the book bag, put it on and ran out of her room. She flew down the stairs. She reached for the knob of the back door.

"Where are you going, young lady?" she heard the familiar voice ask. April froze. She slowly turned her head to the side and saw her father standing there holding his cup of coffee.

FOUR

"**I**. . .I. . .I. . .UM. . . I'm going to Grace's," April said, as she started to feel butterflies in her stomach.

"Well, right *now* may not be the best time for you to be outside," April's father said as he looked out the window at the elephants marching down the street.

April's mother rushed to the door with her cell phone in her hand. Red-faced she said, "Oh no, missy. You are staying put until they figure out what the heck is going on out there." She had one hand on her hip and the other hand that held the phone pointed outside.

Austin came trailing behind his mother. "But, Mom…but, Mom," Austin pleaded.

"END of discussion," their mother declared. April knew that fiery look in her mother's eyes. Her mother was not going to let her out of the house.

April went back upstairs to her bedroom and closed the door. She put the book bag down and pulled out the cell phone. As her fingers pressed the buttons, her heartbeat quickened. *What am I going to do?* Her shaking fingers pressed the 'Send' button.

Grace and Eve answered on speaker, "Hello?" Grace asked.

"Where are you?" Eve asked.

"My helicopter mother won't let me out of the house. Can you guys come here?" April asked.

"I guess we'll have to," Grace said. "My mother is downstairs right now freaking out because of this little elephant parade you created and Michael is at a park with his friend across town. Actually, I may be able to make that work for us. Hmmm...let me see if I can make this happen. I'll call you back." Grace hung up the phone before April could respond.

April took the spell book out of the bag. She ran her hand across the rough leather cover. The raised edges looked like they may have been gold at one point in the past. She opened the book. The binding made a cracking sound and the smell of a cozy library rose up to greet her. She gently turned the pages. The pages were so thin they were almost like tissue paper. April studied the words as she turned the pages. She really wanted to be able to read the book on her own. She told her mother she wanted to learn French. So, her mother bought her a French/English dictionary and signed her up for French classes for the upcoming summer. April used the dictionary all the time.

She turned to a page that had a light pencil drawing at the top. The drawing looked like it was of a person sleeping in a bed. But, there was another drawing next to it that looked like it was the same person standing. The drawing showed the wind blowing and the person with her eyes closed as if she were sleepwalking or flying in her sleep.

Above the drawing, in cursive, the words, *Rêver Magie* were written. April put down the book and reached for her French/English dictionary on her desk. Just as she opened it, her bedroom door flew open. April's heart raced. She jumped off the bed and dropped both the dictionary and the spell book on the carpet. As they fell to the ground she heard a page tear.

FIVE

April looked up from the book to the door and exhaled. "Whew. I'm glad to see you guys," April said to Grace and Eve who were panting in her doorway. She ran over and gave them both a huge hug. Then she gasped.

"Oh no! The *Book of Magie*. I heard it tear." April walked over to it and slowly picked it up and turned it over. Her eyes scanned the pages. Luckily, it was only a small tear at the top of the page.

Eve walked over and looked at the book over April's shoulder. Her eyes narrowed as she looked closer at the page. "Well, shut my mouth."

Grace looked at Eve like she had ten heads. "Please do translate what that means?"

Eve rolled her eyes then looked at April. They both sat down on the edge of the bed. Eve's eyes were as wide as saucers. "April, dear, did you—can you understand what page you were on? Do you understand what you were looking at?"

"Well, not really. I was just about to use my dictionary," April said, looking at the dictionary on the floor. "But then you guys came in and startled me. Wait, how did you guys get over here?"

Grace jumped up with a big smile on her face. She threw her arms up in the air. Grace was so dramatic. It often seemed like she belonged in a play or a movie. "Well, you know me. I always can come up with a plan. My mother was FREAKING out about Michael being across town, since, you know, the elephants came to town. I knew just how we could get over here because your mother wasn't going to let you come to my house. I went to her and said..." Grace walked closer to April. She placed her hand on April's shoulder and looked into April's eyes. Grace blinked a few times and made a concerned face. "...I said, 'Mom, why don't you go get Michael since you are so worried and Eve and I will go to Mr. and Mrs. Appleton's house. We will be safe there.' She completely bought it! She brought us here as fast as she could. Then she took off to go get Michael." Grace's voice became quieter, "I hope she drove safely by those elephants." Grace looked off into the distance.

April raised an eyebrow and looked at

Grace. "You are sometimes a little too tricky for your own good."

"If that ain't the truth," Eve said with a smile.

"Tricky? I'm the tricky one? I'm not the one who put the elephants on the street. By the way, it stinks outside! It smells worse than the bathroom smells after my dad is in there for a while. Those elephants are pooping up and down the street. Everywhere!"

Eve chuckled.

"Anyway, Eve," April said turning to face Eve. "What was that thing you just said about shutting up?" April asked as she furrowed her brow.

Eve tilted her head to the side like she was thinking. "Ohh, you mean when I said, 'well shut my mouth'." She laughed. "You're funny. Well that means...oh never mind what it means. I was just surprised when I was reading this page that you were reading in the *Book of Magie*."

"So, why is that surprising?" Grace asked as she sat on the bed next to Eve and April. Grace was very focused on what Eve was saying.

Eve ran her hand across the torn top of the page where the pencil drawing was of the person sleeping in bed. She lightly smoothed out the crinkled top.

"Well, this page is about doing magic in your dreams. So, April, how exactly did you make these elephants appear? What happened?"

SIX

APRIL passed the book to Eve and looked down at her hands. She started picking at her nails. "I really was trying to help," she said as a lump grew in her throat.

Grace touched her hand. "April, we know that you did not want to do anything bad. Just tell us what happened." April raised her head. Her eyes scanned her room. On the wall, she noticed one of her art projects of an elephant with his trunk raised. She remembered that her mom told her that trinkets or pictures of elephants with their trunks up are good luck. *Oh, Mom I hope you are right. I need some good luck now.* April let out a heavy sigh.

Eve used her one free hand to pat her friend's back.

"Well, in school, my class has been trying to help the elephants, right?" Beads of sweat formed on April's nose. Her new glasses slid down to the tip of her nose. She pushed them back up.

"That's right. And you are part of the Save the Elephants Club too," Eve said nodding her head. Eve put her hands back on the book. Eve and Grace were in the other fifth grade class and they were working on different projects.

"Yes, one night on the *Discovery Channel*, my dad and I watched this documentary about what's happening to the elephants in Africa and Asia. The elephants were so cute and they looked so happy with their babies. But, there are these people that hurt them and kill them. Did you know that in ten years the elephants might be extinct?"

Heat rose into April's face. "Did you know that people are killing them for their ivory tusks? They are just big, harmless animals." April balled her hand into a fist. She pressed her nails into her hand. "They have been on Earth forever. It's not right that people are killing them!"

"Whoa, April, calm down. We agree." Eve assured her.

"We SO agree," Grace made her eyes really big.

"So, in class, I wrote a letter to the President about why we need to do something to help the elephants." April took a deep breath. "Some other kids also wrote letters to the President,

Congress people and other government people," April spoke quickly, without taking a breath.

"Didn't you do that march for elephants a few weeks ago?" Grace asked as she got up and walked to the window.

"Yes! My dad, mom, Austin and I marched to raise money to help protect the elephants," April smiled. "There were so many people there and we raised a lot of money. My mom said we can do the march again next year!"

"That is really awesome that you are an elephant lover and all; but how did we get from you loving elephants to me watching this elephant poop on Mrs. Smith's deck, then go take a bath in her pool?" Grace asked as she pointed out the window.

Eve and April jumped up and walked over to the window. They pushed their heads in front of Grace's to look.

"Oh my," Eve said as she put her hand in front of her mouth.

"Well, in my dream I was flying over them, and thinking about trying to help save them," April shrugged her shoulders.

"By 'save them' you thought it would be best for them to be in our town and not in their own habitats?" Grace asked, raising both eyebrows.

"Why do you have to always be a smart-aleck? I was just trying to help them. And I didn't know that by just dreaming about them I would bring them here!" April pleaded.

"You're right. I'm sorry." Grace said with a smile, looking at April.

"Girls, we should read that spell April opened in the *Book of Magie*," Eve said taking the hands of April and Grace to pull them together.

"Before we read the spell, do you both see

that elephant over there?" Grace pointed across the street.

"OMG, he just sat on and crushed a dog house," Grace laughed.

The dog stood in front of the elephant and barked. The elephant raised his trunk and slowly started to move.

"He's getting up," Eve said. "What is he going to do?"

The dog kept barking and barking. The elephant turned around in a circle. He squatted and took a big poop right in front of the dog. The dog yelped and backed up.

"Well, that's one way to get him to stop barking," April said, as they all laughed.

SEVEN

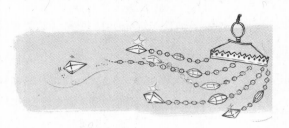

Eve walked over to the bed. She picked up the book and sat on the pink carpet. As she placed the heavy book on the ground, its weight made a muffled thump. April sat on the floor next to her. The plush carpet was comfortable to sit on with her legs crossed. Grace opened the bedroom window.

The smell of the elephants came rushing in with the fall breeze.

"Oh gosh," April said, crinkling up her nose.

"Close that, close that!" Eve fanned the air in front of her nose.

"Not the brightest idea I've had," Grace said. She closed the window and sat on the ground next to the other girls. "So, here we are again. This feels awfully familiar." Grace winked at Eve.

Eve started to read the book and mumbled to herself. April looked up at her ceiling. She was admiring the new chandelier light fixture her dad just put in. She looked at the sun streaming into her room, reflecting light and rainbows off of the crystals. *It looks so nice when the light dances off of it. It twinkles and dances and makes pretty little dancing rainbows and colors around the room.*

The room became very quiet. You could hear a pin drop. Then the chandelier started to sway on its own. And, the crystals were tapping each other making light music.

"The chandelier is dancing," April said,

pointing to it. Eve and Grace looked up. Then the chandelier started swaying faster.

"Why is it dancing faster?" April asked. Then the chandelier started to swing more. The crystals were banging into each other now. The light chiming turned into clanging.

"That is really violent dancing," April said cringing, pulling her shoulders up to her ears.

"Stop saying 'dancing'. I think you are commanding it," Eve said with her hand up toward the chandelier as if she was blocking it just in case it fell. The chandelier swayed harder and faster, banging into the ceiling, and the crystals crashed into each other.

"How do I stop it?" April asked. Her heart raced. "What do I do?"

Eve quickly flipped through the book.

"Eve, quick, it's going to bring down the ceiling," Grace said. Just at that moment, a crystal flew off the chandelier and into April's wall. *Wham*! It left a small mark.

A thin crack was developing in the ceiling from the chandelier's violent sway. *Wham!* Another crystal flew off the chandelier.

"I've got it! I've got it!" Eve said. "Stand up and point at it then say this three times:

"Listen. I command, do as I say,
Go back to your original way."

"I don't want to stand up," April said as she ducked another crystal flying off of the chandelier.

Grace hid from the flying crystals by taking cover under the bed. The thin crack in the ceiling grew longer with each sway of the chandelier.

I caused this. I have to fix this. April took a deep breath and stood straight up. She extended her arm. She pointed at the chandelier and said:

"Listen. I command, do as I say,
Go back to your original way.

Listen. I command, do as I say,
Go back to your original way.
Listen. I command, do as I say,
Go back to your original way."

Poof! It stopped. No clanging. No banging. The chandelier hung perfectly still. It was pretty much the same, except for a few loose wires missing their crystals. April stared at her finger. She slowly brought it down by her side. She swallowed hard. She looked at Eve whose mouth was wide open and eyes were bulging. *OMG! Being a witch can be super scary, but also kind of fun.* A smile spread across her face.

Grace peeked out from under April's bed. Breathing heavily, April said, "Thanks, Eve."

"No problem. I...uh...didn't know I could even read French that fast."

Grace crawled out from under the bed, sat next to Eve and exhaled deeply. She looked in the book and asked, "Now where were we?"

EIGHT

"**APRIL,** please, no more crazy thoughts," Grace pleaded.

"It wasn't a crazy thought. I just thought—"

"No!" Eve and Grace said at the same time.

Oh no! Did Mom and Dad hear all of that craziness? April did a running tiptoe to the door and slowly opened it. She crept into the hall. All she heard was the television turned up really loud.

April heard her brother yell, "OK, Mom. I'm

checking now!" He ran up the stairs and came close to her face. "What is going on up here?"

"Well, I sorta made the chandelier do this thing," April whispered.

"What!" Austin demanded.

"Don't worry. Don't worry. We will figure it out. Just keep them busy and keep the television up loud just in case anything else happens," April instructed.

"I will. But try to keep it down because next time I won't be able to convince them to stay downstairs," Austin said, wagging his finger in her face.

"OK. OK." April said. She walked back in her room. Austin went back downstairs. She closed her bedroom door, leaned against it and wiped the sweat off her forehead. "We have to fix this fast," April said in between breaths.

"Just come sit right here next to me." Eve patted the rug. April sat down cross-legged on the rug. Eve flipped back to the slightly torn page in the *Book of Magie.*

She pointed to the words written in bold cursive writing:

Rêver Magie

"Do you know what this means?"

April looked at the letters. The pretty, fancy letters were written with many loops. They looked like the letters that spell 'The End' in fairy tale books. April shrugged her shoulders, "Something magic?"

"It means 'Dream Magic'." Eve looked into April's eyes. Eve did not blink. Her serious dark brown eyes were locked onto April's. Eve ran her hand down the page. "What this says is that as a witch's powers become stronger, she—"

"Or he?" Grace asked with a smile.

"Yes, or he." Eve smiled back. "He, or she, can make things happen from their dreams."

April swallowed hard. Eve's eyes stayed locked on April's.

"April?" Eve asked. "What did you dream? What were you doing when you were flying over the elephants?"

April looked around the room again. *Gosh, what was I thinking in the dream?* "Oh! That's right!" April quickly looked at Eve, then at Grace. "I was dreaming that I wanted to help bring the elephants to a safe place where they would be safe from the people trying to hurt them. I thought it would be good for them to be in a safe place where they could roam around and a safe place for them to have their babies."

"We get it. You wanted them in a *safe* place," Grace nodded her head as she got up off of the floor and walked over to the window. She looked outside.

"Exactly, Grace!" Eve said as her eyes lit up.

Grace looked at April then at Eve. "Exactly, what?"

"When April thinks or wants or feels something really strongly, and keeps thinking or wanting or feeling that thing, then it happens. Like with the chandelier. Remember, she kept saying 'dancing'," Eve explained.

"And, I kept thinking it too," April jumped in.

"Right," Eve said, pointing at April.

"Well, you have to start thinking and wanting these elephants back in Asia and Africa; because they are not exactly fitting in here," Grace said as she looked out the window.

"I know elephants don't exactly belong in the suburbs," April rolled her eyes.

"Belong is different than causing problems." Grace pointed out the window to the right. "That one over there," she pointed to an elephant that pulled down a tree, and was eating it in the middle of the road. "She looks pretty hungry. She's eating all the leaves and apples off my mom's tree."

Grace's face was pressed against the window. She was breathing so heavily that she was starting to fog up the window. She wiped it away with her hand. Then she pointed down to the left. "That one over there is spraying Mr. and Mrs. Jones' house with their own pool water."

"Oh no!" April put her head in her hands. "What have I done?"

NINE

"APRIL, how about we try what we did to stop the chandelier?" Grace asked.

Eve closed the *Book of Magie.* "That sounds like a good idea." She dropped it on the rug next to her. *Thud*! She rubbed her legs. The book left an imprint on them. "Golly, that is one heavy book," she mumbled to herself.

"What should I say?" April asked as she bit

her lower lip. She started picking at her nails again.

Grace paced back and forth. "How about, 'Please send the elephants back to their natural habitat and please make them safe there.'" Grace said, scratching her head.

"OK." April stood up. She took a deep breath. She walked to the window. She saw an elephant sitting on the hood of her neighbor's car, causing a massive dent. *Oh goodness. What have I done? Fix this! I can fix this!*

She walked over to the window. Her palms became sweaty. She rubbed them on her jeans. She took another deep breath.

Eve stood up. Grace walked over to her.

"I hope this works," Grace said quietly to Eve.

"Oh, I hope so too," Eve replied. Eve was shaking nervously. Grace clenched her teeth.

Both girls held hands and they crossed their fingers.

April pointed toward the elephants on the street. Beads of sweat formed on her nose again. Her glasses slid down. She pushed them back up. Her hand shook. She took a deep breath and steadied her hand. *I can fix this, I CAN fix this, I CAN FIX THIS!* She squeezed her eyes shut. She thought about how calm and nice her street was before the elephants came and pooped everywhere, before they ripped up trees, before they were taking baths in her neighbors' pools.

Her eyes relaxed as she exhaled. With her eyes still closed, she imagined her street clean and neat. She said:

"Send the elephants back to their natural habitat and make them safe there.
Send the elephants back to their natural habitat and make them safe there!

Send the elephants back to their natural habitat and
make them safe there!!
Send the elephants back to their natural habitat and
make them safe there!!!"

Her voice became more forceful each time she repeated the phrase. At a snail's pace, she opened her eyes. She took one, then two steps to get closer to the window. The knot in her stomach grew bigger and bigger each inch she moved forward to look out the window. She swallowed hard then peered out the window as Eve and Grace stayed back.

"Did it work?" Eve asked.

"Are they gone?" Grace asked, sounding unsure.

TEN

AS APRIL peered out the window, she looked down. The beads of sweat caused her glasses to slide down her nose again. She pushed them back up.

"NO!" April cried. The elephants were still there! There was still poop in the streets; and they were still playing in the pools; and there was still one sitting on a car.

Eve and Grace ran over to the window. "Oh,

that is going to leave a dent," Grace said, pointing to the elephant sitting on the car.

April walked around the bed and sat on the rug. She leaned against her bed and hung her head. The book lay next to her. She looked at its hard cover.

Why can't I fix this? What did I do wrong? I'm going to destroy everything! The lump in her throat grew as a tear fell from her eye. Using the back of her hand, she tried to wipe away the tear but instead brushed her glasses off of her face. They fell to the floor.

Grace and Eve sat on the rug on either side of her. Grace picked up her glasses. She used the bottom of her shirt to wipe them off. Eve picked up the *Book of Magie*. She put it on her lap. As she opened it, the smell of the antique pages filled the air.

April wiped off her face with her hand. *I have to find a way to fix this.* She took another deep breath and lifted her head. She looked over at Eve.

Eve's eyes were focused on the page that April was on before. April stared at the picture of the woman that lay on the bed. April focused her eyes more. She noticed something was in the woman's hand. She took her glasses back from Grace and put them on. *What is that?* Her eyes shifted to another picture of what looked like the woman floating above the ground. The picture looked like she was flying. Her hair was flying back with the wind.

April's eyes scanned the French words on the page. She looked up at Eve, who was focused on the words. Her lips moved silently as she read the page.

"Oh, I did not see that before," she said as if she was speaking to the book.

"You did not see what before?" April asked, her eyes still fixed on Eve.

Eve kept reading as though she did not hear April. Her eyes scanned the page faster and faster as her lips moved more and more.

"Earth to Eve?" Grace waved her arms to get Eve's attention.

Eve kept reading.

"EVE?!" April and Grace called at the same time.

"I've got it!" Eve lifted her head. "Geez, since I started hanging out with you gals my French has gotten so much better. I can read it way faster now."

"You've got what? Can we fix this?" April said and held her breath.

Eve smiled.

ELEVEN

Magie de reve

"OK," Eve began. "I think we messed up because I did not read this. This line is very important," Eve pointed to the first line of the second paragraph and read:

"Rêve magique ne peut être modifié par la magie de rêve."

"I love when you speak French. It's so pretty," April smiled.

"Yeah, but what the heck does that mean?" Grace asked with pursed lips.

"I think it means that dream magic can only be changed by dream magic," Eve said. She gave them a huge bright smile.

"OK...what does that mean?" April squished up her face.

"Listen up now," Eve began.

"We have been listening." Grace raised an eyebrow.

"It's just a Southern saying."

"Oh!" Grace and April said at the same time.

"This is our answer!" Eve said, excitedly throwing her arms up in the air.

"Please do explain," Grace said with a fake Southern accent.

Eve glared at her. "It means that you have to be in a dream to change the magic you did in a dream...get it now?"

"Ohhhhh..." Grace and April exclaimed, slowly nodding their heads in unison.

"The light bulb went on?" Eve asked.

"Oh," Grace said with a smile. "It seems, I do declare, that Miss Southern Belle is becoming sarcastic like us." The girls giggled.

"But, seriously now, what do I need to do in my dream? How can I make them go away? I mean, like, go away to a safe place?" April asked.

"Well...um..." Eve looked back down at the book. "I...uh...I think we...uh...might have to get some things first."

"What kind of things?" Grace looked at Eve out of the side of her eye.

April could see Eve swallow hard. "Well, we have to collect three things that were changed or that is a result of the magic that was done." Eve's forehead creased in concern.

"Huh?" April asked.

"Um, for example...maybe like a tree branch, some pool water, and uh...maybe some elephant poop?"

"EWWW! Why does being a witch have to be SO gross!" April said moving her nose around like she could smell the elephant poop.

April felt her stomach turn. She looked down at the book that was still on Eve's lap. She pointed to the picture of the woman's hand that looked to be holding something from the picture. "So, this is an example of the three things you mentioned, huh?" April asked.

"Yeah sorry, honey," Eve said in her sing-song accent.

April took a deep breath. She closed her eyes. *I really hope this works. Being a witch can be hard work. I don't want anything else to be destroyed. I just want everything to go back to the way it was. But then again, being a witch is kinda cool.* "OK, I'm ready," she opened her eyes. "But, how are we going to get out of the house to get the three things?" April asked.

They both looked at Grace.

TWELVE

"**I GUESS** I'm up! Hmm..." Grace said, looking off into the distance. *Tick-tock. Tick-tock.* The ticking of the pink rhinestone-covered clock filled the silence. April stared at the gold numbers on its face.

Tick-tock. Tick-tock. Tick-tock.

April and Eve looked at each other, waiting for the next outburst by Grace. But there was still silence.

Grace rapidly blinked her eyes and turned

her head from side to side. "I feel like I can see the wheels turning in her brain," April whispered to Eve.

"So," Grace said. "Let me just make sure I am clear." Grace squinted her eyes. She rested her chin on her thumb and started to tap her pointer finger on her cheek. Grace clearly watched way too many detective television shows.

"We have to distract April's parents, get outside to get three things the elephants messed up, then get back into the house, and then get April to fall asleep. Is that right?" Grace looked at Eve.

"Yes, ma'am." Eve nodded.

"Just making sure that I have that right. OK!" Grace's eyes lit up as she jumped to her feet. "So, I think, April, you should stay here and keep your parents busy with Austin." Grace looked at April. "Then Eve and I will go to the back door and try to sneak outside to get the three things." Grace motioned to Eve.

"OK," April replied.

"And," Grace continued, "I will bring my cell phone and I want you to carry yours too, just in case we need to text, OK? Sound like a good plan?"

"Let's give it a try," April said as she stood up. She grabbed her cell phone, then put it in her pocket. Eve closed the book and slid it under April's bed.

"I'm going to go downstairs first. I'll go into the living room and distract them. You guys come down the stairs quietly and go through the dining room and into the kitchen. Go out that door and get the three things." April took a breath. "But, before you leave, go under the sink and get some plastic bags just in case you need to pick...uh...anything up," April exhaled.

"Wow, you're becoming a planner too," Grace smiled at April.

Gosh, I don't like hiding this stuff from my parents. Mom just bought me these pretty new school clothes. April looked down at her new jeans. *Then I go and do this. Ugh! And, Dad just let me stay up late with him. He made popcorn for us to watch that movie together. That was so much fun.* April felt her smile melt off her face and turn into a frown. *I'm NEVER, EVER going to trick them again.*

"Ready?" Grace asked.

Her bedroom door opened. Her mother was standing there. "Ready for what?" her mother asked.

THIRTEEN

APRIL'S heart raced as she stared at her mother standing in her doorway. *How long has she been standing there? How much did she hear? She is smiling at me, so I don't think she heard anything. Whew! Answer her. Think of something FAST. Think. Think.*

"I...um...was asking if...if the girls are ready to go downstairs. Yeah, I wanted to see what the news was saying about the elephants, you know?" April swallowed hard. Her palms were wet with sweat. She wiped them on her jeans.

"Well, they are not saying much. They don't seem to know how the elephants got here or where they came from," April's mom said as she walked into April's room. She walked closer to April and gave her a slight hug as she rubbed her head. April hugged her mom back. She always felt safe when she was close to her mom.

"I'm just glad that you girls are safe," her mom said. She gave April a gentle kiss on the top of her head.

Then she looked up at the ceiling. "What happened there?"

April froze. She stepped back from her mom's hug. She just stared at her mom then back at the ceiling. *Oh no. I can't lie to her again. What should I say? What should I say? I'm a horrible daughter.*

Grace jumped to her feet. "Yeah, that looks

like what happened to my ceiling...um...around the ceiling fan after we had that big rain storm a few weeks ago. Remember that storm?"

Eve nodded as her eyes grew wide.

"My dad had to call this guy who went on the roof. Apparently, there was a leak that caused some cracks in the ceiling." Grace stared at Mrs. Appleton as she inspected the ceiling.

"Oh, that makes sense," April's mom nodded. "I guess I should tell your dad to check this out." April exhaled and started to breathe again.

Mrs. Appleton examined the chandelier more carefully. "But, why are there crystals missing?" She touched some of the crystals then a lone wire that looked as if it had formerly held a crystal.

Grace briskly walked to the door. "Um, Mrs. Appleton, could Eve and I please have some, um, juice?" Grace looked at Eve and made her eyes big.

"Oh, yes please, Mrs. Appleton," Eve said putting on her sweet smile. Eve walked toward the door following Grace.

"Oh sure, girls," Mrs. Appleton said. She let go of the wire and walked toward the door. April quickly followed her.

Thank goodness for those girls. They save me every time. But, geez, I have to fix this fast. I really don't like not telling her the truth. One day I will tell her everything, April thought as she closed the door behind her. She checked her pocket to make sure she still had her cell phone.

FOURTEEN

THEY all walked down the stairs, past the front door, through the dining room and into the kitchen. Grace whispered to Eve, "Change of plans. Can you please keep Mrs. Appleton busy? I'm going to sneak out the front door on my own to get the three things for the spell."

Eve looked worried but nodded her head.

Mrs. Appleton was pouring the apple juice while she stood behind the kitchen island. She faced the family room which was right off of the kitchen. She stared at the television as she poured. Eve walked up to her. "So, um...Mrs. Appleton, did you like that jambalaya my mom made for the school potluck dinner?"

Mr. Appleton and Austin were sitting on the couch facing the television. The couch was in front of the kitchen island. Mrs. Appleton's back was to Grace and April. April glided over to the sink and slowly crouched down. She opened the cabinet under the sink, and reached in and grabbed a few plastic shopping bags with handles. Her mom always put them there after she came back from the grocery store. April slowly stood up. She tightly balled them up in her hands behind her back. Reaching behind her, she passed the bags to Grace. The girls quietly crept backwards out of the kitchen. They walked through the dining room and past the stairs. They stopped at the front door.

They heard April's mom speak to Eve. "Yes,

honey. It was great. Your mom, uh, actually gave me the recipe. I was, uh, going to make that tonight but I do not think I will be able to get to the grocery store today." Mrs. Appleton sounded distracted as she spoke.

April could still see her mother staring at the television. The news was showing the elephants marching down many of her neighborhood's streets. They also showed picture after picture of the elephants causing destruction. The elephants were making a massive mess of their neighborhood; doing everything from eating and breaking down trees, to stepping on cars, to pulling down traffic lights and stop signs.

Grace looked over at the television. They could both hear the news announcer telling everyone, "Stay inside! For your safety, do not go outside!"

"Oh gosh, I better be careful," Grace said

as she reached for the knob to the front door. Her face was ghost-white as she quietly opened the front door. She usually had a perfect golden tan all year. But, at that moment, she was as white as a sheet of paper. April held her hands as Grace held the bags.

"Sorry, Grace," April said. She took another deep breath.

"Sorry for what?" Grace asked as she furrowed her eyebrows.

"Sorry for this." April grabbed the bags, quickly pushed Grace to the side, and ran out the door. Grace tried to grab April's arm, but she was already out the door. April turned back to look at Grace who was staring at her as she walked toward the street. April mouthed, "Sorry. *I* have to fix this." April turned around to face the street.

I have to fix this. I made this problem. Grace did not do anything wrong and I can't put her in danger. I have to make it right before my mother notices I'm gone. And, I hope... April took a huge breath. *I hope I am safe and nothing bad happens to me.*

FIFTEEN

APRIL'S heart raced with each step she took. The ground continued to shake as the elephants walked. The closer she came to the street the stronger the poop smell became. She wiped her nose as if that would push the smell out of her nostrils.

Acid built and climbed up her throat. She swallowed hard trying to push it back down. Her stomach churned as she walked over to one of the trees that the elephants uprooted.

She leaned down and picked up a small branch from it. *One down, two more things to go. What else can I get?* She placed the branch in her bag.

As she stood up, she looked between two houses, and saw an elephant taking the water out of her neighbor's pool and spraying the water everywhere. The yard was flooded. She walked between the houses toward the elephant.

The closer she got to the elephant, the bigger he seemed and she had to tilt her head further back to see the top of his head. She was breathing with her mouth open trying to get in as much air as she could. There she stood, with just the pool between her and the elephant. She looked at him. She studied his grey, wrinkled skin. He had so many folds and flaps she could not count them.

Everything I read says they are big, harmless creatures. He's not going to hurt me. He's

not going to hurt me. He's not going to hurt me.
She took a huge, deep breath trying to calm
down a little bit. The elephant stood on his back
legs then came crashing down to the ground.
BOOM! April's heart raced so fast, each beat
vibrated in her throat and head. She just
stared at him, but then noticed something out
of the corner of her eye: a pretty purple flower
that washed over to her on the flooded grass.
She bent down, picked it up and put it in the
bag. The elephant stared at her for a moment
As their eyes met, April stopped breathing. *Is
he going to do something? Is he going to come
over to me?* Then he looked away and went back
to spraying the pool water everywhere.

Ding! April heard her cell phone go off. She
reached into her pocket and pulled it out. It
was from Grace:

"R U OK?"

"Gr8. Just gr8..."

"No, seriously. Are you OK?"

"I've got 2 things. Looking for #3. Suggestions?"

"Branch?"

"Got that."

"Uh...poop?"

"Must I?"

"Thinking..."

"Is Eve keeping my mom busy?"

"Yep. They are now onto how to make muffuletta sandwiches."

"What?? Well keep her busy, k?"

"Sure thing. And next time...don't push me."

"I know. I'm sorry. Won't happen again."

"Hurry back."

April looked around. She saw that same elephant still sitting on the car, and a few still tramping down the street. Right in front of her, on the side of the road, was a huge pile of elephant poop. *Should I? Ugh! I swear I'm never EVER doing a spell again. Well, I really didn't mean for this one to happen.* She walked closer to it. The smell was so strong that she coughed a little. She covered her nose with her arm and kept walking closer.

She opened a new bag and checked it for holes. With one hand in the bag, so she did not have to touch it, she reached out to grab some of the poop. It was hot and steamy. The mushy warmth made April gag. She scooped it, turned it inside out and quickly tied it as tight as she could. She ran back to her house and through the front door. She closed it behind her. *I'm glad Grace left the door cracked open!*

"Who is at the door?" she heard her father ask. She heard steps coming closer to her. *Oh no! What should I do? What should I say?*

SIXTEEN

APRIL opened the bathroom door in the front hallway and ran in. She closed the door behind her. Her father came around the corner and knocked on the door. "April, did I hear you come through the front door?" her father asked.

"Uh, uh, oh, oh—"

"What is that smell?" her father asked, sounding grossed out. "April, honey," he asked carefully, "do you have a... stomachache?"

"Uh, uh, yes! YES! I have a BAD

stomachache!" April replied. She looked down at the plastic bag with the elephant poop in it. She exhaled and her shoulders dropped. When she inhaled and realized how stinky it was, she pinched her nose.

April groaned and moaned like she was in pain. Her dad turned the knob on the bathroom door. April put her foot in front of the door to stop it from opening all the way. The door cracked open but not enough for him to look in, "Honey, do you need help? Are you OK?"

"Oh no, Dad. I'll be OK. I think, uh, that smell from the elephants got to me."

"OK, honey. Do you need any medicine?"

He is so nice. He takes such good care of me. I'm so lucky. "No thanks, Daddy," April smiled. She knew that he liked it when she called him Daddy, like when she was a little girl.

"OK. I will give you a minute," her dad said. He pulled the door closed and walked away.

April dropped the bag of poop on the floor. She looked at her hands. *Ick! That poop was so squishy, hot and steamy. Gross!*

She washed her hands then reached in her back pocket to pull out her phone to text Grace.

I'm in the downstairs bathroom. My dad thinks I have a stomachache. I have to get upstairs so we can do the spell.

April heard Grace saying, "I'm going to bring April something for her stomach." Grace's voice grew louder with each word.

"Be careful in there. It certainly smells like she has bad gas or something!" April's dad said to Grace as he chuckled a little.

Grace lightly tapped on the door. "I followed the smell. Are you in there?"

"Yep." April sounded like she had a cold because she was pinching her nose shut.

"They are both watching the news. Come out and we'll go upstairs." Grace cracked the door. She stuck her head in. "OMG, that *is* a horrible smell!" Grace wrinkled up her nose and quickly stepped backwards.

April came out of the bathroom. She picked up the bag and extended her arm to hold the bag as far away from her body as possible.

Grace also pinched her nose so she did not have to smell the horrible poop. Sounding like she had a cold too, she said, "I'm going to get Eve. You go upstairs and get ready to do the spell...ewww."

April went up the stairs, into her room and closed the door behind her.

She put the bag of the three things on the rug in the corner of the room. "Phew!" She fanned her nose. She knelt down and pulled out the *Book of Magie* from under her bed. She opened it to the page she had been on before. Her fingers glided across the small tear in the page. She tried to un-crinkle it. *I really do not want to do anything bad again. I only wanted to help the elephants. Maybe Eve's grandmother is wrong. Maybe this is a curse and not a blessing.*

I have to make this right before someone tries to hurt the elephants because they are destroying our town.

April's bedroom door swung open. Eve and Grace stood there squeezing their noses. They both rushed over to April and sat on either side of her.

"Oh, honey. You look sad. Don't worry. We'll fix this." Eve smiled at April.

"Maybe this isn't a blessing," April said as her voiced cracked.

"What are you talking about? Maybe you shouldn't have wished in your dream to bring them here; BUT, you could try dreaming that they are protected in their natural habitats. That would help to keep them safe." Grace tilted her head so she was looking right into April's eyes.

"That would be like being a fairy godmother to the elephants, right?" Eve continued.

April took a deep breath.

"As I read the spell, you could definitely NOW dream that you protect the elephants in their homeland. You could do the spell like a bubble of protection around each of these elephants," Eve pointed outside toward the elephants.

April smiled. She put both her arms around her best friends. "You girls are the best! Eve, what did the rest of the spell say? I want to get them back to their homes and get our home all cleaned up."

"Well, it says that you have to lay down and fall asleep," Eve took the book from April's lap and put it on her own. "And, while you lay down you have to hold the three things. So..." Eve cleared her throat and looked at April and then at the plastic bag. "You have to hold that bag in your hand."

April looked across the room at the bag as it sat in the corner. *Ugh!* April nodded.

Eve continued, "When you lay down you have to say:

> 'As I lay down to sleep,
> A sleep that is very deep,
> I make a wish to un-do,
> The spell I did as I flew.'"

"How does it know what or who I did the spell on?" April asked.

"It's magic. The universe knows," Eve tapped her friend on the leg to reassure her.

"OK. I trust you," April said to Eve.

"You have to say that out loud three times, then keep repeating it in your head until you fall asleep. You said in your dream that you were flying, like the picture, right?" Eve pointed to the picture of the woman flying over something as she pointed.

"Yeah." April nodded.

"When you fall asleep and you are flying over what you want to undo, you have to replace your thoughts with what you want to have really happen. So, instead of thinking you want the animals to be protected, you have to think, 'I want the animals to be protected in their natural habitat.' Get it?" Eve asked as she raised an eyebrow.

"I think so," April replied.

SEVENTEEN

"**READY**? Ready to do the spell and make these elephants go back to their home?" Eve asked April.

April stood up. Her heart started beating faster. She walked over to the plastic bag. She bent over to pick it up. As she stood back up, she felt a little light-headed. With another deep breath, her head cleared. She walked over to her bed and lay down. She swallowed hard.

Grace and Eve stayed sitting on the rug.

They turned around to face the bed where April lay. Eve was nervously playing with the corner of the page of the *Book of Magie*. April heard the sound: *flick, flick, flick*. April's palms were sweaty. They were making the handle of the plastic bag slippery.

April blinked quickly. She took another deep breath then closed her eyes. She could not figure out how she was going to fall asleep. After all, she had just woken up and she was so stressed about all that she had done. She heard Grace and Eve whispering but could not make out their words. Then, the spell popped into her head as if she had known it all her life. That freaked April out a little; but she kept breathing deeply and tried to be as calm as possible.

She let out a large exhale and said:

"As I lay down to sleep,
A sleep that is very deep,
I make a wish to un-do,
The spell I did as I flew."

April took another breath. Her eyes stopped fluttering. They remained closed. Her heart stopped beating so fast. She felt her face relax.

"As I lay down to sleep,
A sleep that is very deep,
I make a wish to un-do,
The spell I did as I flew."

Silence. She did not hear anything. No more elephants walking. No more Grace and Eve whispering. Nothing. April repeated the words over and over and over again in her head.

Poof! She was back in her dream where she was flying over the elephants. She felt the wind caressing her face. Her hair was blowing in the warm breeze. Looking down, she saw the trees and swaying grasses. She saw lots of adult and baby elephants roaming on the land. The clean, dry air filled her nose as the sun warmed her skin. She smiled.

I want the elephants to be protected in their

natural habitat. I want them to be safe here and roam in their own land. I don't want anyone to hurt them. As she flew, the air glided over her fingertips. She gestured at the elephants and thought, *I hope they are safe here on their land roaming free. I want them to stay here but be protected.* She repeated this thought over and over again. She took another deep breath, looked up and focussed her eyes. *Where am I?*

EIGHTEEN

APRIL opened her eyes. *Am I back in my room?* She looked at her ceiling. Her eyes moved to her chandelier. It was perfect. There were no missing crystals. There were no hanging wires. She looked at her wall. There were no dents from the flying crystals. She listened but did not hear anything. Silence. The sweet sound of birds chirping filled the air.

She jumped out of bed and looked out her bedroom window. Nothing. The trees were intact. They stood up straight with green, red, orange and brown leaves. Leaves were rustling on the trees and leaves were dancing on the street as the wind blew.

Her neighbor's car was perfect. No dents. She pressed her face into the screen to look down the street. No elephants. She took a deep breath in through her nose. The crisp fall air smelled fresh. No elephant poop. She looked down at her hands. Then she looked in the corner of her room. The bag of three things was gone.

She looked over at her desk. Her cell phone was sitting there. She picked it up and texted Grace:

"The elephants are gone! YAY!!! And, my chandelier is fixed...that's weird. And, where are you?"

Grace replied:

"April? What's wrong? What elephants? What was wrong with your chandelier?

Only you would have a chandelier in your bedroom, btw. And what do you mean? I'm at home!"

"Huh? The elephants we just did the spell on and the chandelier I made dance... remember?"

"What spell? Dancing chandeliers? Elephants? That must have been a dream. Eve just got to my house. Are you still meeting us at the park?"

April lifted her head and looked out the window. She felt all the blood leave her face. Her jaw dropped. She slowly scanned her room with her eyes. *What just happened? Did I just rewind to before the elephants were here? I get it! By undoing the spell, I started the day over!*

"OMG!" April fell on her bed. Her arms went limp. She swallowed. *I just went back in time. And I am the only one that knows about this.*

She sat up, picked up her cell phone and texted back to Grace:

"I'll be over in a little bit. I'm going to lay back down for a sec."

"Yeah, sounds like you may need a little bit extra sleep. We'll see you down there l8r."

She put the phone back on her desk, took a deep breath and sat back down on her bed. She walked out her room. The muffled sound of the television and her parents talking echoed upstairs.

I guess I'll get some breakfast before I head over to Grace's house. Skipping down the stairs, she walked into the kitchen, and heard the morning news show that her parents normally watched. As she poured her cereal, she heard the announcer say,

"In happy news today, because of good people around the world, the elephants of Africa have a new large reserve extending 30,000 square kilometers for their protection. Private and corporate donations, and Save the Elephants Walks have raised enough money to create the protected space..."

April looked at her mom who was smiling

at her. Then she quickly turned to her dad who was grinning from ear to ear. Her mom walked over to her and gave her a hug.

"Look what you helped to do," Mrs. Appleton said, squeezing her daughter tightly.

"Look what WE did," April said as her face warmed. Her mom beamed with pride.

"OK. I better get to my next task." April let go of her mom and walked back to her cereal. She quickly shoveled a spoonful into her mouth.

"I gotta go gra gre gra," April said.

"April, don't talk with your mouth full," her mother scolded.

April swallowed.

"Sorry. I have to get to Grace's house. Eve, Grace and I have a project to do for school." April quickly finished her breakfast and cleaned her dishes. As she went up the stairs, she paused, looked back, and watched her parents working in the kitchen. She smiled and then quickly ran upstairs to get dressed to meet up with her best friends.

OMG...
IS HE A WITCH?!

APRIL Appleton lay in her bed on her side looking out the window at the foggy night sky. *I'm so happy the elephants are safe.* She looked at her chandelier. *And, I'm so happy that fiasco is over. I wonder what my next adventure will be?* She closed her eyes.

Bam! April jolted awake. She sat straight up. *What was that?* She swung her legs over the side of her bed and hopped to her feet. She scurried to the window. She pressed her face against the glass trying to see, but the fog was as thick as pea soup. April could barely make out a boy standing at the end of her driveway. He looked shadowy and ghostly in the foggy night. He seemed to be looking up at the large tree that stood near their house.

"Fall!" he said in a stern tone.

April heard a loud cracking sound which made her jump. Her heart was racing. She was breathing quickly through her mouth. Her heavy breath fogged up the window and she could not see out of it. She used her hand to wipe the window clean. *Where did he go?* She couldn't see anything. She opened the window. She looked left. Then she looked right. Nothing. The tree appeared to be fine but it was impossible to make out any details. She felt a chill go up her back as the damp air entered the room. She closed the window and turned around.

"Am I dreaming again?" April asked. "Wait, now I am talking to myself." April's eyes scanned the dark room. Everything was in place. Her stuffed animals, the chandelier. She looked under her bed and the *Book of Magie* was still there.

"I have to be dreaming," she reassured herself, got back in bed and fell back asleep.

***

"Oh NO!" April's eyes popped open. "Abbey! Abbey! Can you come down here?" She heard her father yelling up the stairs to her mother. She heard her mother go running down the stairs.

"Honey, what's wrong?" April heard her mother say. A pit grew in April's stomach. She sprang out of bed and ran to the window. She covered her eyes. *Please say it was a dream.*

Please say it was a dream. She squeezed her eyes shut and tightly squished her face while holding her breath. She slowly relaxed her face and then opened her eyes. *Please, please, please. It must have been a dream.*

As her eyes adjusted to the bright sunshine pouring in her window, she saw it. Her father's car was crushed by a massive branch from the tree near their driveway.

"OMG... Is he a witch?!"

✶ ABOUT THE AUTHOR ✶

Talia Aikens-Nuñez dreamed of being a meteorologist as a child because her head was always in the clouds. It was her imagination and her fun-loving, second-grade daughter that inspired her to write her OMG books about an accidental little witch. She and her husband live on a river in Connecticut with their daughter and son.

Talia's other books include:

OMG... Am I a Witch?!
Escucha Means Listen

★ TREASURE HUNT ★

How much do you remember about the story?

1. What danger did April want to save the elephants from?

2. What does it mean when an elephant's trunk is up?

3. Which two continents do elephants live on?

4. What excuse did April give her father for being in the bathroom?

5. What language is the Book of Magic written in?

6. What three things did April need to reverse the spell?

7. Did the spell work the first time?

8. What fell on April's father's car?

9. Do you think that April caused that branch to fall?

★ WORD SEARCH ★

```
Q  T  S  B  Y  D  E  N  F  L  I  Y  A  P  E
A  N  Q  L  X  W  A  R  B  O  P  W  F  O  C
I  A  X  Y  R  I  K  N  U  D  I  G  R  O  A
S  H  P  E  M  T  S  F  G  T  R  E  I  P  R
A  P  V  N  Q  D  W  P  C  E  N  E  C  L  G
Q  E  W  Y  N  T  S  H  O  B  R  E  A  V  M
R  L  R  E  I  L  E  D  N  A  H  C  V  M  P
I  E  I  H  O  G  U  T  S  P  E  L  L  D  S
V  R  K  O  L  G  F  J  X  W  S  Z  T  A  A
F  Y  G  G  C  I  G  A  M  E  N  C  V  N  N
K  S  U  T  K  L  X  M  V  L  T  E  O  O  X
Q  C  E  J  N  C  R  T  Y  C  I  C  L  J  W
A  F  N  D  B  X  E  F  S  M  E  R  B  W  L
R  E  S  E  R  V  E  E  P  V  C  A  P  W  P
D  E  Y  C  E  P  A  U  M  W  B  L  S  A  Y
```

ADVENTURE	AFRICA	APRIL
ASIA	CHANDELIER	DANGER
DREAM	ELEPHANT	EVE
FRIENDS	GRACE	MAGIC
POOP	RESERVE	REVER
SAVE	SPELL	TEXT
TUSK	WITCH	